This book belongs to:

. . . .

Copyright © 2014 Acamar Films Ltd

First published in the UK in 2014 by HarperCollins *Children's Books*,
a division of HarperCollins Publishers Ltd, 77-85 Fulham Palace Road, London W6 8JB

1 3 5 7 9 10 8 6 4 2

ISBN: 978-0-00-752982-7

Based on the script by Lead Writers: Ted Dewan and Lucy Murphy and Team Writers: Mikael Shields and Philip Bergkvist.

Adapted from the original books by Ted Dewan and using images created by Acamar Films, Brown Bag Films and Tandem Ltd.

Edited by Neil Dunnicliffe.

Designed by Anna Lubecka.

Bing ™

Ducks

HarperCollins *Children's Books*

Round the corner, not far away,
Bing is feeding the ducks today.

Hello Bing.

Hello Flop.

It's a sunny day and Bing,
Flop and Sula are at the park.

They've brought bags full of
food for the **ducks**.

"Look," says Bing.
"A duckie!"

"That's not a duckie," says Sula.
"That's a pigeon."

Bing asks Flop why the pigeon
doesn't fly away.

"Because the statue is very,
very good at staying still,"
says Flop.

"Oh, statue still,"
says Bing.

As they run to the pond, Bing and Sula shake their bags and sing.

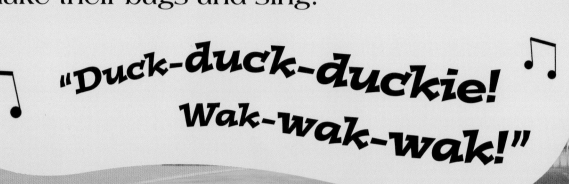

"Duck-duck-duckie! Wak-wak-wak!"

Scared by the noise,
the ducks on the pond
all flap away.

Flap!

Flap!

Quack!

Bing is disappointed.
"Oh, why have the ducks gone?"

"I know, Bing!" says Sula.
"Let's give them some food."

Bing throws a **big** handful of food on to the pond. He waits.

"Look, Bing!" whispers Sula. "There's one."

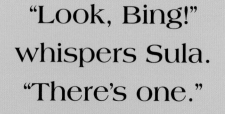

"Where?!"

shouts Bing.

The duck **bobs**
down under
the water.

Flop points at the statue
and whispers,

"Remember Bing,
statue still and
shhh. Then the
ducks will come."

"OK!" Bing whispers back. He stands statue still.

Up pops the duck again from under the water.

"A duckie!"
yells Bing.

Whoops!

The duck flaps
off again.

"Why won't that duckie come to me?" asks Bing.

"Because you're all NOISY, Bing. He gets scared when you go

blulalulah!"

says Sula.

Bing watches Sula. She is quiet and still and feeding lots of ducks.

"Aw, Sula's got all the duckies!" says Bing.

Bing **throws** some food on to the pond.

A little duck swims over from Sula's
side and **gobbles** it up. Ooh!

Bing gets excited and throws **all** of his duck food into the pond. The **whole** bag!

Floof!

All of Sula's ducks swim over to Bing.

But someone else has seen the food...

"Hey!"

Splash!

The ducks scatter.

"I got a BIG duck!" says Bing.

Sula takes a step back. "Bi-ing, that's not a duck. That's a goose! And he's eating all the food!"

The goose **flaps** his wings and **jumps** out of the water. He is coming for more food.

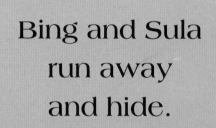

Bing and Sula run away and hide.

Flop takes Bing's empty bag. He blows into it,

POP!

and scares the
goose away!

"Ohh, all of the ducks have gone," says Bing.

"All of the ducks?" asks Flop.

A small duck hops on to the path.

Bing and Sula stay very still. Statue still.
And very quiet. Bing holds out some more food.
The duck comes closer. It nibbles at the food!
"It tickles!" giggles Bing.

Nibble!

Nibble!

Nibble!

"Good for you, Bing Bunny."

Hi!

We went to feed the **ducks.** But Sula had **all** the ducks...

so Flop said 'stay statue still'. Then the ducks would come to me too.

But a **big goosey** came and it went

waaarggghhh

and that was scary.

So Flop went

pop and goosey

flew away.

If you're very quiet and statue still, then the duckies will come.

Feeding the ducks...

it's a Bing thing.